KAY THOMPSON'S ELOISE

Eloise's Mother's Day Surprise

STORY BY **Lisa McClatchy**

ILLUSTRATED BY **Tammie Lyon**

Ready-to-Read

Aladdin

NEW YORK · LONDON · TORONTO · SYDNEY

ALADDIN PAPERBACKS
An imprint of Simon & Schuster Children's Publishing Division
1230 Avenue of the Americas, New York, NY 10020
The text of this book was set in Century Old Style.
Manufactured in the United States of America
First Aladdin Paperbacks edition March 2009
2 4 6 8 10 9 7 5 3 1
Library of Congress Cataloging-in-Publication Data
McClatchy, Lisa.
Eloise's Mother's Day surprise / story by Lisa McClatchy ;
illustrated by Tammie Lyon.—1st Aladdin Paperbacks ed.
p. cm. — (Kay Thompson's Eloise) (Ready-to-read)
"Artwork in the style of Hilary Knight"—T.p. verso.
Summary: Nanny takes Eloise shopping for the "best best best" Mother's Day gifts.
ISBN-13: 978-1-4169-7889-3
ISBN-10: 1-4169-7889-5
[1. Shopping—Fiction. 2. Gifts—Fiction. 3. Mother's Day—Fiction.
4. Plaza Hotel (New York, N.Y.)—Fiction. 5. Hotels, motels, etc.—Fiction.
6. New York (N.Y.)—Fiction.]
I. Lyon, Tammie, ill. II. Thompson, Kay, 1909–1998. III. Title.
PZ7.M47841375Elf 2009
[E]—dc22
2008049718

Oh, I love, love, love, love Mother's Day!

I am Eloise.
I am six.

I live in the Plaza Hotel
on the tippy-top floor.

"A box of chocolates for you.
And a rose."

"I have one last thing."

"Wait, Nanny," I say
when we are done.

We hand them to the manager to send them to Mother.

Nanny, Weenie, and I
take our presents back
to the Plaza.

Only Saks Fifth Avenue
will do. Mother must have
the best, best, best!

"Just one more thing,"
I say to Nanny.
"A new hat for Mother."

"Only Tiffany will do,"
I tell Nanny.
Mother must have the
best, best, best!

"Now we shall buy her a ring," I declare.

I pick the reddest roses
because Mother must have
the best, best, best!

"Next, we buy flowers,"
  I say to Nanny.
"This vendor will do!"

Mother must have
the best, best, best!

Nanny takes me
to Godiva.

Weenie and I love chocolate.
So does Mother.

Nanny lets me
decide what to buy.
"First, we shall have
to buy chocolates," I say.

Oh, I love, love, love
to shop!

Nanny says, "Do not forget your spring hat and your purse, Eloise!"

We put on our
springtime best.

We put on our sunglasses.

Weenie always goes
shopping with me.

This is my dog.
His name is Weenie.

Nanny says we must, must, must go shopping today. It is almost Mother's Day!

Time for mothers.

It is spring.
Time for sunshine.
Time for flowers.